# GREY MOTHER MOUNTAIN

## ELYSE RUSSELL

Copyright © 2022 by Elyse Russell

All rights reserved.

No part of this book may be reproduced or transmitted in any form or by any means, electronic or mechanical, except for the purpose of review and/or reference, without explicit permission in writing from the publisher.

Cover design copyright © 2022 by Niki Lenhart
*nikilen-designs.com*

Published by Water Dragon Publishing
*waterdragonpublishing.com*

An imprint of Paper Angel Press
*paperangelpress.com*

ISBN 978-1-957146-26-3 (Trade Paperback)

FIRST EDITION

10 9 8 7 6 5 4 3 2 1

*To my Evie,*
*who made me love dragons again.*

# GREY MOTHER MOUNTAIN

THE WIND WHISPERED THROUGH THE BRANCHES and ran soft fingers down the wrinkles and grooves in Neela's ancient face. She closed her eyes and tilted her head to the sun, listening. She heard the Boula birds shrieking in the distance, and the yapping of a mother rosy-tailed fox as she tried to keep her cubs in line. Children played nearby, digging in the dirt and flinging it at each other.

A subtle shift in the air temperature warned Neela of an impending storm. She turned to her daughter-in-law, Mua, and smiled.

"It will rain soon," she stated softly.

The two women sat companionably upon the hill near the forest's edge. Behind them, the forests stretched up into the higher mountains. Their village was situated on one of the lower foothills, and had been there for many generations. In the opposite direction, a great green valley spread out before them like a giant bowl. The mountains ringed their home like the arms of a protective grandmother.

The Ke'lan people had all that they needed here. The forest provided timber, hunting, and shade. The valley was the perfect place to graze their giant yaks, from whom they got milk, hair to weave into mats and blankets, and strong backs to pull their plows. They grew many kinds of vegetables, and there was a crystal-clear stream that ran right down through the middle of their village and into a small pond, where the children could swim on hot days.

Neela had grown up here. She had climbed those trees nearby when she was little, had splashed with the other women in the stream on bathing days, and had birthed her children in her hut near the center of the village. She could look around and see her entire life spread before her. Her parents and husband had been burned on their platforms in the valley below, and now their bodies were forever a part of the sky overhead.

Someday soon, the village would carry her body down to the valley and send her up to the heavens in a million floating pieces, carried on the broad back of the smoke yak. Her great-grandchildren would look up at her on clear days, and beg her to send rain during droughts. In time, they, too, would join her up there.

*That it how it will be,* Neela thought.

Neela was so close to that final rest. Her joints ached, and moving was difficult. She didn't have many teeth left, so her food had to be pounded into a pulp for her to eat. Sometimes, she could feel pains in her chest. It would not be long. She would be with her sky family, looking over and after her earth family.

"Would you like me to help you inside for supper now, Grandmother?" Mua asked, addressing Neela with respect.

Neela sucked on her remaining teeth as she considered. "No," she finally responded, slowly. "We will make a fire here. I will tell stories for the children tonight, and then I will sleep beneath my husband."

Mua nodded and shifted her great bulk as she stood. She gathered her basket-making supplies and wandered away toward the huts.

Neela watched the children as they ran in a small herd down to the water. They jumped in enthusiastically, little bare bums flashing, making Neela chuckle. She had always loved children.

That night, the entire village gathered around a great fire, constructed on the hill before Neela. Food was passed about, and families cuddled together. A newborn nursed at her mother's breast, and a young, courting couple stared at each other without shame. All was as it should be.

That night, Neela told the story of the Great Grey Mother. Dragons had not flown these skies in decades, and it was thought that they had gone extinct. The last sighting by their tribe was before Neela was even born. There were, however, plenty of stories about them to tell, and Neela's favorite was of Grey Mother.

She cleared her throat, and everyone went still. No one ever wanted to miss a word of one of Grandmother Neela's stories.

Neela laid her withered hand on the shoulder of the nearest child, a little girl. She pointed in the direction she wanted the child to look.

"Do you see that great mountain there, child?" she asked.

"Yes, Grandmother, I see it."

"That is Grey Mother Mountain, the oldest mountain in the world. It has stood watch over us for thousands of years, and will do so for thousands more. But it is more than a great mound of stone. The mountain is alive. It breathes puffs of smoke into the air sometimes, from deep in its belly. That is because the Great Grey Mother sleeps in the stone womb of the mountain.

"Grey Mother is the largest dragon that ever lived. She is the same color as the mountain itself. She was born from a rockslide, when an enormous chunk of the mountain slid off the northern face. When that stone shattered on the ground, the little pieces flew up into the air and formed great wings that carried the Grandmother of all dragons into the sky. She gave an earth-trembling roar that caused chasms and cracks to erupt between the other mountains, creating the ravines where the healing plants can be found today.

"Grey Mother had many children, and they spread across the sky and rested on the mountaintops. Their screeches and roars echoed through the clouds. Some were green, some were brown, and one was even known to have been golden in color.

"They were fierce, with rows of teeth like daggers and talons that could easily split a man in half. Their tails were long and tapered, and they would crack them in the air like whips to challenge each other. But none of them ever grew to the same enormous size as their mother.

"She could eat a quarter of a yak herd in one attack. One of her feet could crush a hut to pieces. She could have easily borne ten people on her back. When she lashed her tail, the resounding crack would startle birds away for miles. She was power incarnate.

But then, one day, before I was even born, a foreign king offered rewards to anyone who could bring him a dragon's head. Our tribe watched as hunting parties came into the mountains to take down first the smallest dragonlings, and then the larger ones. They took their heads for their king's collection.

"It was a dark day when they took down the Grey Mother's largest son. The golden dragon fell, the male that shone as brightly as the sun when he took to the skies. He was shot down with great, mobile ballistas. Where he landed, a small portion of the forest was crushed and remains clear of trees to this day.

"He was killed not far from here, and so the tribe saw and heard his downfall. They say that the moment he was shot and roared in pain, there was an answering bellow from Grey Mother Mountain. The great grey dragon emerged to block the sun, and then swooped down upon the hunting party, to eat several men.

"They managed to shoot her with the ballista, and her wing was torn so badly that she had to flee and crash elsewhere. We heard the hunting party looking for her, and one of our scouts trailed them, but she was never found. She had gone back inside the mountain with her broken wing and heart. And she has not been seen since. She is part of the mountain now."

*Grey Mother Mountain*

All was quiet around the campfire as Neela finished her story. A few of the children looked at the outline of the great mountain, looming in the twilight sky. Even the ones that had heard the story before were caught up in the awe of imagining a great dragon coiled beneath the slopes.

"What happened to the king?" one of them suddenly asked.

"The hunting party took the golden dragon's head back to him, and we have not seen his people here since. They live on the other side of the mountain range. Traders have wandered through and talked about the king's grandson, who would be getting on in years now. They said that the throne the current king sits upon was crafted from the golden head of Grey Mother's largest son. He sits in its mouth every day, and the golden scales were soldered back onto the bones after the flesh rotted away.

"And so, because of one man, the dragons were extinguished."

"But ... couldn't the dragons breathe fire?" another child asked.

"No. The females could spit a poisonous liquid that was highly flammable. The males could spit acid that would melt a man's face off. But it was never in quantities large enough to engulf an entire hunting party. It was meant to incapacitate their prey."

There was silence as everyone pondered this. Several people were gazing at the sky, no doubt picturing leathery wings beating powerfully overhead. Neela had often done the same. She had had a very happy, fulfilling life, but ...

*I would have loved to have seen a dragon,* Neela thought. *Just once.*

She'd heard all of the stories, and had absorbed them with enthusiasm since childhood. When she was a little girl, she had imagined going to Grey Mother Mountain herself and finding the Grandmother of all dragons.

Neela told other stories that night, until all of the children were sleepy-eyed and slumping onto their mother's laps. Slowly, people got up and left the fire to return to their huts. Finally, it was only Neela, Mua, and two of her granddaughters. The four women slept under the stars that night, whispering each other to sleep.

• • •

Launette was the daughter of a King, the wife of a King, and the mother of a King. And yet, whenever she was about to enter the throne room, she had to stop to control her trembling. She couldn't decide what was more terrifying: the awful throne, made from a dragon's head, or the man who sat upon it. It didn't matter that the man was her own son. She hadn't raised him.

As a future King, he had been taken from her at birth to be raised by a circle of the "wisest" men in the nation. She hadn't been allowed to even nurse him. She had only been allowed brief, scheduled visits, during which she had to act as a Queen, and not as a mother.

It was the way their kingdom had been for centuries. If a King was to be manly, he must be taken early from his mother and raised by men. He had a different nursemaid each day, to discourage attachment. A King must be strong, not sentimental.

And so, Queen Launette did not feel as though she even truly knew the man who sat upon the throne, though he had her hair, nose, and height. She felt love and grief for that infant that had been taken from her fifty years ago, but could not equate that poor, squalling thing with this hard-hearted man.

King Reginald was forever struggling under the reputation of his grandfather, who had been a fearsome man, on and off the battlefield. He'd been a slayer of dragons, and a conqueror of worlds. Reginald's father, and Launette's husband, hadn't sat upon the throne for very long.

As Launette walked toward the throne, leaning heavily on her gilded walking stick, she braced herself for the pain that the low curtsy would cause her. Arthritis was taking a heavy toll on the old woman. But she had been summoned, and King Reginald would never allow anything but the most scraping, bowing obedience — even from his own mother.

Launette had to fight to stay steady as she lowered herself toward the ground. Her curtsy was not as graceful as it used to be, but was still acceptably low. Reginald looked down at his mother with glassy grey eyes, and made her hold the curtsy for a bit longer than was necessary before waving his hand to dismiss her.

*You cruel, cruel boy,* Launette thought.

She was careful to keep her face blank and dignified as she walked to her seat on a long bench behind the throne with the other royals. She sat beside her granddaughter, Blina.

Blina was only fourteen. Girls in the royal family were allowed to stay with their mothers until they were given away in marriage at age fifteen. Launette had had five girls, and all of them had left her on their fifteenth birthdays to live in foreign lands. She rarely, if ever, saw them, and it took a toll on her. It felt, at times, that it had taken years from her lifespan.

Launette knew that she was dying. Glancing sideways at Blina, she found herself hoping that she wouldn't have to live long past the girl's birthday. It was only weeks away, and then Launette would be alone. She'd have to watch one of her girls leave again. But this time, there would be no one else there when she turned around.

After the endless petitions and grievances, Launette's backside felt numb and her spine was in agony.

The leader of a recent scouting party into the mountains was the next person to approach the throne. Flanking him were two younger men, each carrying baskets. Within one basket was a collection of what appeared to be plants, while the other contained lumps of ore.

"The foothills are rich in iron and silver ores, Your Majesty," the man said. "And there are a great many medicinal plants growing throughout the forest. The wood is sturdy and beautiful, and there is a large valley with a lake and a stream that would be a good location for your hunting keep."

*Hunting keep? He's never been interested in the mountain land before.*

King Reginald had always said that the land there was far too rocky and useless. Apart from hunting down the dragons, the focus had always been to the east, to conquer others and their wealth. Beyond providing protection at the city's back, the mountains had thus far escaped his notice.

*But no longer, it seems,* thought Launette.

"And the mountain tribes?" the King rumbled.

"There is a tribe squatting in the valley, but they could be dealt with, should your majesty wish it."

The King thought for only a moment, stroking his beard. Then he waved his hand dismissively.

"Take care of it," he commanded. "I want the work to begin on the hunting keep as soon as possible."

"Shall we keep any of them for slaves?"

"I have enough slaves."

• • •

Neela could feel death approaching. She assumed that it was coming only for her, and so she began to prepare her funeral garb. Other women would come and silently sit next to her to help her weave a new cape to put over her tunic. It would be belted with a rope woven of the pink and green sweetgrass that grew in abundance along the edges of the valley.

A headdress was crafted of strips of leather, and then Neela brought out a carved wooden box. Inside it was a collection of feathers that she had been gathering for years. Every native species was represented, and she had kept only the finest specimens. There were great plumes and soft, downy feathers. The stiff flight feathers of the mountain eagle were the largest and most colorful, with their indigo hue fading to sky blue at the tips.

Neela used twine to tie the feathers to the headdress. Some stuck upward like a crown; others hung down on strings of varying lengths to frame her face and cascade over her silver hair.

The next day, having prepared all of her funeral garb, she gathered her family around her for a feast. She helped make bread for the last time, and they had mashed yams and fermented yak milk. The hunters had brought down a large boar, which roasted on a spit. For dessert, there were berries baked into cakes and covered with sugar.

The children played games, the adults drank and told stories, and Neela sat like a queen in the middle of it all in her new outfit. It was a celebration of her life, and of the part she'd played in the history of the tribe. She told stories of her life, and glanced often at the sky, which would soon be her new home.

With every minute, she felt death creeping closer on its pale, spindly legs.

• • •

Launette found Blina crying in her bedchamber. She immediately sat and wrapped her arms around her granddaughter and waited patiently for the girl to talk. She ran her fingers, swollen with arthritis, through Blina's shining black hair and made soft shushing noises.

"I d-don't w-want to m-marry him!" Blina wailed.

Launette didn't blame the girl. She'd seen the portrait of the man to whom she was betrothed. The man was at least thirty years the girl's senior, and already had an heir. To make matters worse, his kingdom lay across the sea. After she set sail for his kingdom, she and Launette would never see each other again.

"I know, my girl," Launette whispered reassuringly. "I know."

• • •

Death finally arrived the morning after Neela's funeral feast. But it didn't come for *her*.

The first sign of the impending attack was the flight of the Boula birds. Large flocks of them were startled into the air on the horizon, and were flying over the village in a frenzy.

Neela stood, still wearing her funeral garb, and squinted toward the far trees. Though it seemed her entire body was failing in her old age, one sense that had not been dulled by the years was her sight. Miraculously, Neela still had the eyes of an Ela, an enormous bird of prey.

The racket of the squawking birds brought other villagers out of their huts with confused expressions on their faces. Children halted their games as hundreds of flitting shadows passed overhead.

A strong wind blew to Neela from the place the birds were fleeing. She scented metal and horses. With a sinking feeling in her core, she went to stand on the highest hill in the valley and raised her arms up over her head. Wind swirled the hair and feathers about her face. The sky began to darken.

Down the hill, the yak herd grew restless. They began to mill about, snorting in confusion at the change in the weather and the strange scents coming to their nostrils. One of the calves made a frightened keening sound.

Mua and her son, Kalo, appeared suddenly at Neela's side.

"What is it, Grandmother?" Mua asked respectfully. "What approaches? What has frightened the animals?"

"They smell steel," Neela responded solemnly. "Steel, sweat and blood."

Neela tilted her head back and closed her eyes as the clouds overhead grew heavier and darker. The first patters of raindrops hit her skin and dribbled down the deep furrows and crags in her cheeks.

"Tell the able-bodied to prepare to fight. Tell the elderly to get the children out of the valley."

"But Grandmother, who is it?" Kalo asked. "Who has come?"

"They come from the land of the king who killed the dragons."

Mua blanched and hurried off to find her children.

Kalo's thick eyebrows drew together in concern. "They're too close," he whispered, more to himself than to Neela.

Neela did not respond, but kept her hands upturned in the air and called for the rain, hoping to slow the invaders' progress and cover the tracks of the escaping children. Behind her, she heard the warriors assembling. She knew her people so well that, without turning, she could imagine how they would appear. There were forty of them, with fifteen riding yaks.

The rain was coming down in sheets when the first line of invaders broke through the trees and into the valley. They rode great armored warhorses and bore weapons that the Ke'Lan had never seen before. Neela gritted her teeth as the sky continued to weep, and more and more men emerged. Hundreds.

In that moment, Neela knew. She knew that the village would be completely destroyed. Their only hope would be to stall the invaders long enough for the children to escape. But neither the children nor the elders could move very quickly. Thunder started to rumble a low warning.

The assembled riders across the valley stood perfectly still in the downpour until they received a signal from their leader. Then, they began to charge. The earth rumbled beneath the enormous hooves of their horses, echoing the roaring thunder overhead. The storm was almost upon them.

At the sight of that line of armored warriors charging, a few of the warriors ran. The Ke'Lan had had peace in the valley for generations; they were accomplished hunters, but not fighters. They had never faced such a threat. None of them had ever killed another human being.

Neela drew up as much energy as she could, pulling it from the ground and the sky, from the grass and from her own bones. Her eyes crackled slightly with electricity as she slowly lowered one of her arms to point a finger at the oncoming horde.

The lightning strike hit the very center of the front line. Horses shrieked. The smell of burnt flesh drifted to the Ke'Lan, even through the pouring rain. Men fell to the mud, and there was a moment of pure chaos. Neela felt her knees buckle underneath her.

That one blast of energy had taken everything she had. As Neela lost consciousness, she heard Kalo scream, and focused with painful clarity upon the face of the approaching enemy commander. That face burned itself into her brain with its hatred and fury. The man's teeth were bared, and he was preparing to throw a spear.

Neela's cheek hit the slick, cool grass and she heard the whistle of the spear and the thud as it hit Kalo in the middle of his chest. Then everything went black, and the old woman lay at the mercy of the pounding hooves.

• • •

Launette couldn't sit still that evening, knowing that the next morning would bring her one day closer to Blina's birthday and subsequent departure. Something about that night felt ominous. Launette had never been a superstitious person, but she felt like the air crackled with menace. Something bad was coming. She knew it in her old bones.

• • •

The morning light was harsh and not at all warm. It shone down on Neela's face. She groaned as awareness returned to her, along with a rush of severe pain. Without opening her eyes, she tried to assess what was wrong with her. It felt as though she had a bruised rib and broken wrist. Her leg throbbed, as well. A cut on her head had bled into her hair. She could feel it matted against the back of her scalp. On top of all of that, she felt drained. So much magic. She'd used so much.

Neela's eyes opened slowly, and her pupils dilated to let in some of that cold light. At first, she saw only the blue of the sky, spread out over her like a blanket. She blinked slowly and watched as a wispy cloud of smoke floated past her vision. A bird soared high overhead, too high for her to identify the species.

Shakily, Neela lifted a hand and brought it to her face. Mud was caked to her skin, and blood too. She touched her forehead and grimaced. Her temples throbbed with a headache. Why did her head hurt so badly?

Neela coughed and then cried out softly in pain as the movement jarred her bruised rib. She wondered what had happened.

*Why am I injured? Where is Mua?*

Turning her head to the side, Neela focused on a patch of tall grass in front of her face. A beetle twiddled its way up a blade and then flew away once it reached the top. Then, her focus slid through the grass to the face on the other side.

The old woman bit down on a scream as she beheld the blank stare of Kalo. A spear was still lodged in his chest, and blood had run out of the corners of his mouth and dried into dark lines, like tattoos. His eyes were blank. As Neela watched, a fly landed on the white part of one of his eyes and crawled across the pupil.

Gulping down panicked breaths, Neela turned her head to the other side. The dead littered the ground all around her.

*My people.*

With a moan of terror, Neela tried to sit up. Then she immediately lay still when she caught a glimpse of canvas tents nearby. The enemy was encamped within her village.

Her mind raced.

*Did anyone survive? Can I escape and somehow search for the children?*

A group of laughing men interrupted her thoughts. She looked in the direction of the sound to find that they had begun looting and burning the huts. No one was looking at her. The tree line was within crawling distance, if she could only move without attracting notice.

Inch by inch, Neela scooted painfully backwards until she was within the shelter of the trees. Once there, she collapsed behind a thick clump of bushes to catch her breath with one hand pressed to her aching chest. The men had been too busy destroying the village to notice that one corpse was not really a corpse.

Neela watched, tears pouring down her face, as her home was destroyed. She counted the bodies of her people and started the list of names of the dead in her mind. There lay one of her daughters ... there her grand-niece ... there one of her grandsons ...

As she watched, one of the soldiers laughed as he pissed on the body of a young woman ... the best friend of one of her granddaughters. Bile worked its way up her throat and she vomited into the dirt.

*But the children,* she thought, *and the elders ... where are they?*

Then she looked up and she saw them.

All of them, every single child and elder, hung from the branches above her, swinging in the slight breeze. The branches creaked with their weight. A few trees away, Mua's corpse rotated slowly until Neela could see her purple face ...

Neela vomited again. The list in her mind was complete. She was the only survivor.

• • •

"Please stand still, miss," the seamstress said through a mouthful of pins as she worked at fitting Blina for her wedding gown.

Blina didn't care, though. She wouldn't even look at the dress, but rather stared absently out the window. There was no bridal joy in her dark eyes.

Launette watched from a settee near the window. She sat with her back ramrod straight, though it hurt her. She sat like a queen, because the King was also in attendance.

"This alliance will bring great wealth and security to our kingdom, girl," the King barked. "So you'd better not look so horse-faced when you walk down the aisle."

• • •

Neela crawled away from the village with a heavy heart. She knew that she had no chance of survival on her own in the forest. The nearest Ke'Lan village was two mountains away. She'd never make it. It would be best to simply stop moving and let death take her, as well.

But somehow, she couldn't stop. She kept creeping along, slowly moving away from the carnage. Some force drove her onward, one she could not yet put a name to.

When she had gained some distance from the dead village, she heard a rustling in the foliage behind her. Holding her breath, she looked around frantically, certain that she'd been discovered. She waited to hear the sound of a sword sliding from its scabbard. Instead, she heard a huffing noise, followed by a deep snort.

With relief, Neela realized that one of the yaks was staring at her. It, too, had escaped into the woods. It wore wearing a saddle, marking it as one of the riding yaks that had borne a warrior the previous night — a warrior that was now dead.

Neela made shushing noises as she crept across the ground toward the yak. The shaggy animal lowered its great head to blow a hot, steamy breath across her face. It obediently remained still as Neela grabbed onto its legs and fur to brace herself as she stood. Once she was on her feet, she took several deep breaths, trying to fight the looming unconsciousness from the pain.

When her vision had cleared, she gave the signal to the yak to lay down so she could clamber into the saddle. It sank down to its knees for her. With a lowing noise, the beast rose again and obeyed her command to head in the same direction she had instinctively been crawling: toward Grey Mother Mountain.

Neela found a water skin tied underneath the saddle. She immediately lifted it to her lips and drank the warm water. She hadn't realized how parched she was. At least with the giant feast they'd had, her belly wasn't empty yet. She had enough energy, and magic still hummed through her veins. Though she'd used a lot of her power to call forth the lightning strike during the attack, she knew that it was not yet depleted.

After all, nothing fueled magic quite like rage.

• • •

Neela wasn't sure how she had the strength to find her way to the base of Grey Mother Mountain. She was old, weak, injured, and, she could sense, would die very soon. And yet, she sat atop her yak, staring up at the legendary peak. Now, she just had to find the way in.

She closed her eyes and breathed out slowly. Her magic was connected directly to the air. She could feel her way around the entire mountain if she concentrated.

Magic had always been part of Neela's life. She was born a witch, with the magic of air and weather. Witches were rare amongst her people, but not unheard-of. Stories went back to the dawn of time that told of witches that could talk to animals, manipulate water, and even heal wounds with a touch of the hand. Neela would have appreciated the healing touch at the moment. She reached up to touch the blood crusted on the back of her head, and lamented absently that her headdress was gone. It must have been lost in the attack. All those feathers that she had gathered since she was a little girl ...

Of course, the sorrow of losing the headdress was minimal compared to ...

*Do not focus on those sorrows,* she told herself with a small shake of the head. *Not yet.*

By breathing deeply and sinking into herself, Neela could feel where the air went *inside* the mountain. There were several caves and tunnels.

*But which one leads to a cavern large enough to house to a dragon?* she wondered.

When she found a large tunnel only a mile away, halfway up the mountain, Neela immediately directed her yak towards it. The foliage was thick and the slope steep. Combined with her declining physical state, they made for slow going. The yak was strong, but tired, and lumbered up the mountain with laborious steps. Foam dripped from its mouth. Neela reached to snap a branch from a tree along the way.

*This will serve for a torch,* she thought.

The mouth of the tunnel was partially caved in. Neela could see that it was once indeed large enough for a dragon to crawl through. Now, though, there was just enough space for her to ride the yak inside. The beast was hesitant to enter the darkness, but moved forward at Neela's sharp prodding.

She fumbled through the saddlebags until she found a skin filled with a sticky paste. It was made from a rare plant that grew in a nearby ravine, and had the very useful quality of burning very slowly and producing a bright blue flame. This she spread liberally over the end of the branch she'd secured. Then she wrapped it with a shred of fabric and laid it across her lap while she fished through the saddlebags again, this time for flint.

Three strikes of the flint produced sparks that took immediately to the fabric, and then to the sticky paste. Neela held her new torch aloft and pushed her knees into the yak's sides, urging it onwards into the tunnel. The daylight slowly faded at their backs, but the blue flame allowed them to see a few feet in front of them.

The tunnel went down a steep slope, and the yak had to traverse large, hardened piles of old guano from recently-extinct bats, as well as stalactites and stalagmites. Some of them were only inches away from meeting each other to form columns.

After what Neela estimated was about ten minutes, the yak suddenly stopped stock-still. The abrupt cessation of movement startled Neela, who raised the torch higher and squinted into the darkness.

*What spooked the beast?*

The yak gave a strange lowing sound and backed up a step. Neela tried nudging it forward, but it wouldn't heed her signals. With a sigh, she slid slowly to the ground and landed on very shaky legs. Biting back a gasp of pain, Neela grasped the reins and yanked on them as she walked forward, towing the reluctant yak along behind her.

They'd only gone a few steps when a warm breeze blasted them in their faces. A breeze ... that came from *inside* the mountain tunnel. A small smile played across Neela's thin, cracked lips. The yak tried to bolt, but the old woman's grip was iron. Again, she held the torch higher to cast the blue light further. It fell on a line of more stalactites.

Except then, the line of stalactites *shifted*. It moved slightly from one side to the other. That was when Neela realized that they weren't stalactites at all.

• • •

A storm blew over the city. It rolled in with a ferocity that tore shutters off windows and tossed chickens out of yards. Within the castle, Blina ran barefooted down the halls until she reached her grandmother's room.

Blina had always been terrified of thunderstorms. The rumble of the thunder and flash of the lightning sent her into hysterics as a young child. Now, at nearly fifteen, she still sought out the comfort of Launette's arms. Launette had always been the kindest person in the princess's life.

The guard outside her grandmother's door stepped aside to let her into the dowager's apartments. Blina hurried to the giant four-poster bed, where Launette was already sitting up with open arms to receive her. The girl buried her face into her grandmother's shoulder.

Launette patted Blina's back.

"There, there, child," she whispered.

Lightning temporarily lit up the room. The thunder crashed only seconds later, and Blina whimpered pitifully. Launette got up to light a candle. Its warm glow provided some comfort, at least.

Then, to distract her granddaughter, Launette began to tell stories.

Stories of dragons.

• • •

Neela barely had time to step aside before the gaping maw shot forward. The yak screamed in terror before it was silenced with a crunch. Those enormous teeth sliced through the yak's flesh quickly and with sickening ease; the animal was swallowed whole, and the great grey snout withdrew.

Neela immediately followed, keeping her arm steady. She found that she felt no fear. It was not bravery that kept her from trembling in the presence of the terrible monster: it was hopelessness. She had nothing left, and so she was not afraid. There was only one thing left that she wanted.

Stepping forward, Neela looked up and saw that the ceiling sloped up as the tunnel opened into an enormous cavern.

Another hot breath hit Neela in the face, this time tinged with the scent of blood. Setting her jaw, Neela turned in the direction the hot air had come from. Her voice, when she spoke, was the voice of a Queen.

"Great Grey Mother," she boomed, "I seek your aid."

A deep, dry chuckling sound came in answer. Neela hadn't known that dragons could laugh. Then she saw two black, glittering eyes in the blue dark. The Grandmother of all dragons stared right at her.

"WITCH," came a rumbling voice from the dragon's throat. "WHAT MAKES YOU THINK I WOULD AID YOU?"

The mouth opened wide again, and the bloodstained teeth drew nearer. Neela set her jaw in determination.

"Because I know why you are still alive," Neela said.

The approaching teeth hesitated. A drop of sizzling drool fell to the floor of the cavern. Neela kept her eyes focused on those of the dragon. She heard the scrape of giant talons against the stone, and the shifting of a mighty body somewhere in the darkness beyond.

The dragon was silent. She moved her head to the side, bringing one eye up close to examine Neela. The old woman saw herself reflected on the shiny black surface, holding the blue torch. She looked like hell.

The grey scales that covered the creature were enormous. Some of the larger ones above the eye were the size of a yak's hoof. Neela wondered just how big the dragon was. She'd been large and ancient in the stories ... but it had been at least a hundred years since then. Though she couldn't have been eating much, the Grey Mother had to have grown in size. It was the nature of dragons; they never stopped growing. In fact, Neela wondered if the Grey Mother had grown too large to even fit back out of the tunnel.

"AND WHY IS THAT, WITCH?" the voice snarled.

"For vengeance," Neela responded. "Your mother's heart aches for vengeance."

The menacing growl that came in answer shook the very ground beneath Neela's feet. Still, she held her ground. After a moment's hesitation, the dragon withdrew. She settled back into the darkness and Neela heard her lay her great head down on the ground.

With a grunt of pain, Neela shuffled forward, shedding light over the curled form of the dragon. The Grey Mother's head was as large as one of the huts in her ruined village. Her enormous neck encircled a clump of what appeared, at first glance, to be rocks. As Neela came even closer, she saw that they were eggs ... or had been eggs, once.

She reached out the gnarled hand that wasn't holding the torch aloft to touch one of the eggs. It was as cold as ice. Long dead. Petrified. She looked up at the Grey Mother's nearest eye with pity and understanding.

That eye was open and watching her, and it looked suddenly very tired. The fury had drained from it. Neela heard the dragon take in a breath. The sound of the inhalation was a loud *whoosh,* followed by a gust of hot air that pushed Neela back a step. It reeked of death and yak.

Each egg was the size of a small child; twelve of them in all. The Grey Mother's chest rested right next to them, her neck curled around them protectively, as though they were still alive and she was just waiting for them to hatch. Since there were no other dragons alive, she must have been guarding her dead young for over a century.

"LEAVE ME. A DRAGON MUST DIE WITH ITS HEART."

"Your heart?" Neela whispered.

She glanced down at the petrified eggs. A mother's heart always lay with her children. Her eyes grew steely.

"They are not your heart, or you would have died upon them already," Neela stated flatly.

The dragon snarled, but Neela continued.

"No, Grey Mother," she said. "If you wish to die with your heart, you must avenge your golden son."

"WHAT DO YOU KNOW OF MY SON?"

"I know that they took his head and it sits in the throne hall of the twisted king beyond the mountains. I know that the flesh was boiled from his skull and that now, a tyrant sits inside it. I know that your son is now only a trophy — a royal seat."

The Grey Mother roared with fury. The ground shook so violently that Neela fell against one of the eggs. She pushed herself back up to stand as the last echoes abated. Pebbles fell from the cavern ceiling and skittered across the ground.

Neela watched in amazement as a giant tear fell from one of those glittering eyes. As the wetness slid over the scales on the Grey Mother's face, it rinsed away some of the dust that covered her, revealing a darker grey underneath.

"WHY?" the Grey Mother cried.

"Because they are a people without heart. They covet, and they take. If it is beautiful or powerful, then they must possess it, no matter the cost."

The eye came right down to Neela's level again.

"WITHOUT HEART."

"Yes. And they have taken your heart and mine because of it."

"YOUR HEART."

"Yes, my heart. My heart was with my people. The invaders wanted our land, and so they rode out of the trees on metal horses and took it. Every man, woman and child was slaughtered. They hung our babies in the trees."

The Grey Mother snarled again.

"BUT YOU LIVED."

"Yes, I lived. I wish I hadn't. But now, I have one purpose. I have one task yet left to me in this life, before I can part for the skies."

"VENGEANCE."

"Yes, Grey Mother. Vengeance."

The dragon blinked heavily as she considered Neela's words.

"WHAT CAN YOU DO, WITCH? YOUR POWER IS NOT SO MIGHTY."

"Fury fuels magic. And fury is all I have left."

Neela could almost see flames flickering in the depths of the dragon's eye — flames that were far darker than those currently dancing on the end of her torch. She wanted to harness them, and make them burn for her.

"FURY. YES."

"Do you still have fury, Grey Mother? Do you have the fury to avenge your golden son's slaughter?"

"YES, WITCH. I, TOO, HAVE ONLY FURY."

"And fury fuels magic. We have the same enemy, Grey Mother. Shall we destroy them together?"

"SUCH VIOLENCE. WOULD YOU TAKE THE CITY? THERE ARE YOUNG IN THAT CITY."

"They would not spare my young. Why should I spare theirs?"

The dragon practically purred with pleasure at those words. Neela knew from the stories that dragons savored violence and vengeance. They valued retribution and viciousness. They lived to hunt and destroy.

"Will you hunt one last time, Grey Mother? Will you hunt with me?"

The eye flared wider, and the Grey Mother finally lifted her head off the ground. Her long neck snaked upwards, out of the light of the torch, then her face dipped back down into the blue aura around Neela, and she touched her enormous snout to the old woman's face. The scales felt warm and rough against Neela's skin.

"I WILL HUNT WITH YOU, WITCH. OUR FURY WILL ENVELOPE THEM ALL."

• • •

The village had been sacked and the bodies burned. The Commander was pleased with the quick work that his men had made of the project. Trees had been felled, and mining had begun. Stones were being hauled to begin construction on the hunting keep. Some of the men resided in what villager's huts hadn't burnt down during the attack. Others stayed in tents. By the end of the month, they would have more secure shelter.

The Commander heard a whip crack and turned to watch a team of horses hauling a wagonload of stone, their sides coated in a thick lather. Behind them came another wagon, pulled by two yaks that they'd managed to capture from the forest. They were hardy beasts.

One of the wagon drivers threw the Commander a glare, but diverted his gaze quickly once he realized he was being watched. The men were resentful of the Commander, because he hadn't allowed them to keep any of the women for sport. But to the Commander's viewpoint, he would sooner have let his men rut with sheep. At least then, there would be no risk of half-animal offspring.

The villagers had been so primitive as to hardly be recognizable as people. They had looked similar to the attackers, apart from different hair and skin, but the way they had acted was far from civilized. It had been a mercy, really, to put them down and end their miserable existence. Now the valley could be put to much better use.

A distant rumble made the Commander frown and look to the sky. He hoped another storm wasn't on the way. That last one had been a real monster. And what were the odds that his line would get struck by lighting in the middle of a charge? It made him jumpy. He'd been far too close to the men who had been roasted alive in their own armor.

Another rumble sounded. The skies were clear, though. The Commander's frown deepened. What was that sound? Where was it coming from?

His question was answered a moment later when the nearest mountain gave a shudder, and then a part of it started to fall. The Commander's eyebrows flew up to his scant hairline and he watched in terror as the mountain *moved*.

A sinking feeling filled the Commander's gut. He had men stationed on that exact part of the mountain. They'd been assigned the task of mining ore. But those rocks had fallen right where their camp would be …

Men began screaming all around him as more rocks tumbled down the side of the mountain and a roar shattered the air. The Commander's eyes widened as two great wings stretched out from the mountain and beat the air with powerful strokes. A hellacious beast rose into the sky, dark grey against the blue.

"DRAGON!!!" the Commander yelled.

It was impossible. The dragons were all dead. And yet there, spiraling into the air before them, was an impossibly large specimen. Dust and rocks fell from its great wings as they shook free. Another thunderous cry issued from the reptile's mighty throat.

The commander had a realization: they didn't have any ballistas.

"ARCHERS!" the Commander called.

It was no use. Well-trained as they were, his men had never been prepared for a damned dragon. Pandemonium ensued. A horse ran past, whinnying frantically. Several men ran to hide in the huts, while others disappeared into the trees. The Commander went to get his bow.

He knew it was futile. He knew he didn't have a chance of bringing down that massive beast, even as he notched an arrow and his eyes tracked its approach. As the dragon flew closer, it came down nearer to the ground, and the Commander was able to see that there was something on its back ... no ... some*one.*

He drew the arrow back and held his breath, then loosed it when the dragon was within range. He missed. And then the dragon opened its mouth. The Commander felt the wind from its wings. A black liquid erupted from the back of the monster's throat, spraying across the valley. It landed on the Commander and drenched him in its foul smell.

He only had a moment to cough and splutter before he saw something small and bright blue fall from the dragon's back. The Commander watched it curiously as it plummeted to the ground. Was that a ball of ... fire?

• • •

Neela had made tiny pellets of the sticky, flammable paste. She had a tiny piece of the still-burning torch, shielded from the wind by some of the Grey Mother's neck frills where she clung to the dragon's back. Apart from breaking out of the mountain, the Grey Mother had flown very smoothly, to make it easier for Neela to hold on and stay on her back.

Staring at the blue flame, Neela took one of those pellets, quickly lit it, and dropped it, only barely singeing her fingers. It winked out of sight over the side of the dragon, and then ... that glorious blue hit the liquid that the Grey Mother had just vomited upon the men. And the blue spread.

It spread so quickly that none of them had any time to contemplate what was happening. The air filled with screams as the men were engulfed in cerulean and indigo flames. The Grey Mother banked gently and then circled, allowing Neela to see all of the destruction as it unfolded beneath them.

The huts were on fire. Horses were on fire. The trees were on fire. That entire scene of carnage was being burned alive. The stain was being removed from the land of her people.

Neela smiled grimly. It was a start.

• • •

Blina's betrothed was due to arrive any day. The birthday and wedding celebration would take place in a little over a week's time; preparations were already under way. The dress was completed, the menu finalized, the invitations returned, and the decorations for the main hall being created. Launette had overseen all of it.

Launette had caught Blina staring at the portrait of her intended more than once. It was displayed prominently in her room, by order of the King. Whenever Blina looked at it, her fingers began to twitch. And no wonder — the man had a heartless look to him. His mouth was cruel. The painter had done their best to smooth over the man's flaws, but Launette had heard that his skin was splotchy from drinking heavily, and that he had suffered from the pox as a child, which had left his face scarred.

None of this would matter much to Launette, though, if she knew for certain that he would treat her Blina well. But she knew nothing of the kind. In fact, she feared greatly for her poor granddaughter, though she did her best to hide it. There was nothing either of them could do to change her fate.

• • •

Neela began gathering the storm before they even reached the city. It built behind them as a massive thunderhead, roiling with the combined fury of the two ancient females. There would be no stopping this storm once it was unleashed.

The sky turned a sickly yellow.

• • •

When Launette heard the servants tittering nervously about the weather, she sighed and put down her embroidery. She didn't want yet another storm to hit them. Launette stood on creaky knees and walked over to the window. Resting her hands against the smooth stone sides, she leaned out slightly to get a view over the city.

Everything was cast in a jaundiced hue, and the largest storm cloud she had ever seen was gathering on the horizon. Wind was already tearing the flags from the spires and spinning them away into nothingness. Shutters were being slammed, and bells of warning were being rung, alerting everyone to get inside.

Launette glanced nervously at the thatch roofing in some parts of the city. They'd been lucky with the last storm, in that lighting hadn't struck to start any fires. But with a storm this large ... she just fervently hoped that the rain would be torrential enough to put out any fires before they took root.

"Grandmother!" Blina cried, making Launette spin around to face her.

She held her arms open for the shaking girl and enveloped her in her embrace.

"Come," she said. "Let's move away from the window."

They hadn't made it more than a few steps toward the chairs before they heard a strange, loud noise building outside.

"W-what is that?" Blina asked, eyes wide with fear.

Launette waved to the girl to sit down and rushed back to the window. It sounded like a strange growling, like no beast she'd ever encountered, but it seemed to be coming from the storm.

Then she saw the first funnel cloud start to form. She stood in terror. Only once before had she seen a tornado. She'd been at sea when the crew had spotted water spouts forming in a distant storm. They'd horrified her. She'd imagined that they were the long necks of terrible monsters, looking for ships to suck up into their gluttonous stomachs.

She stood frozen for a few minutes, staring at the forming funnel, when she saw something strange.

Something was coming out of the black clouds.
Something enormous.
Something with wings.

• • •

The storm now fed itself. Neela and the Grey Mother had stirred it into such a fury that funnel clouds began to spiral, dropping long, grey legs down to touch the ground. Neela could feel that there would be five large tornadoes hitting the city within minutes.

She could see the entire spread of the "civilization" in front of her. And there, like a great sow, lay her primary target: the palace. Beneath her, the Grey Mother twitched and trembled with fury and excitement. The entire world was her prey.

Once they were over the edges of the city, the Grey Mother began spitting small amounts of the noxious fluid from her mouth, targeting any open fire. The moment it hit those fires, it spread out far too quickly for anyone to put out.

On the way over, Neela had made a handful of little pellets of the sticky paste, and she was now lighting them on fire and dropping them upon the thatch roofs, and into the splatters of dragon spit. Within minutes, the entire poor section of the city was aflame. Blue, yellow and orange licked up the sides of every building. Lastly, Neela threw the remnants of the torch itself over the side, along with any other belongings that were weighing her down.

Her hands completely free, she grabbed onto the spines on Grey Mother's back as tightly as she could. From this point onward, the flying would not be so smooth.

At the signal, the Grey Mother stopped coasting and gave a powerful beat of her wings while simultaneously bellowing out a terrifying war challenge. The roar was echoed by screams throughout the city. She banked hard to circle a guard tower before slamming into the top of it with her hindquarters. Rocks and debris flew in every direction, and more than one guard plummeted to his death in the fiery streets below.

They took out two more guard towers before altering their course for the palace. By that time, the storm was upon the city. The five funnel clouds, now fully-formed, began dancing through the streets, whipping livestock and walls about as if they weighed nothing.

The winds buffeted the Grey Mother's wings, and Neela struggled to hold on. She knew there was no saving the city from the flames or the tornadoes. Anyone who wasn't already dead would be shortly. But none of that would mean anything if she didn't destroy the palace. The King must die — and all of his young with him.

The fury had left her chest hollow. She'd poured everything she had into the storm around them, and now felt weightless and empty. It was time to call on her most powerful weapon: lightning.

When combined with the fury of the dragon beneath her, there was plenty to feed to the magic. Neela's eyes shone supernaturally. Electricity crackled through her bloodstream and sparked at her fingertips. She pulled it all toward her, every particle of energy in the storm around them, and became its nexus. As the Grey Mother brought her within range of the palace, they both unleashed their hell upon it.

• • •

Launette held Blina's face in her hands as the floor beneath them rumbled and cracks spread across the stone. The girl was hysterical; tears streamed from her eyes and over her grandmother's fingers.

"Please, gramma!" she pleaded. "Please, I don't want to die! Not like this! I'll marry him, I swear! Just don't make me die like this!"

The girl had lost touch with reality. Launette was pulled her towards the doorway, thinking to get down to the dungeons, where they might be safe from the tornados. But just at that moment, a gust of wind blew in through the narrow window that was so strong, it blew out every single candle flame in an instant. The two women became engulfed in darkness. Blina began to whimper loudly.

Over the whimpering, Launette could hear the constant roaring of the tornados, the crashing of buildings, the rumble of the thunder, and something else: the occasional bellow from the throat of an enormous, vengeful creature.

Launette thought suddenly of that awful throne that her son always sat upon. The skull of a dragon. This was their punishment for taking that head. She knew it in her bones. So many lives were being lost, because their Kings couldn't refrain from taking whatever they wanted.

The darkness was lit up so magnificently the next moment that the two women were nearly blinded, and then the ceiling caved in.

• • •

Lightning strikes struck the ancient building from every angle. Neela was lit up with the power. It came from her eyes, from her wide-open mouth and from her fingers. It lit up her chest from within, making a glowing lantern of her entire body. Tower after tower collapsed beneath the lightning strikes as the great dragon fought the winds to keep the witch in place over their target.

At last, the center of the palace began to cave in upon itself with a mighty groan. Neela's light went out.

• • •

The King almost made it to the dungeons before the entire palace came down. Almost, but not quite. He, too, was crushed like an insignificant insect beneath the wrath of the witch and her dragon.

Flames swept over the ruins like waves on the sea.

• • •

As soon as the magic left Neela's body, she died. Her body slid off the side of the Grey Mother and fell down, down, down, into the roaring ruins beneath. The Grey Mother let out a cry of torment at the sight of her last friend's body falling, and tucked her great wings in to follow it.

Neela's body landed in the palace courtyard and was swallowed by flames. With a final, heartbroken bellow, the Grey Mother landed on top of the witch's body.

She paid no heed to the flames that began to crawl up her body as she folded down over the remains of her friend. She curled her great neck around the ruined body, cradling the dead with her entire being, just as she had cradled her petrified eggs for the past century.

*Grey Mother Mountain*

The dragon became completely engulfed by the flames, but lay silently as she was burned, and closed her eyes in exhaustion.

The smoke carried many ashes to the ancestors in the sky that day.

# ABOUT THE AUTHOR

Elyse Russell has been writing since she was seven. She loves stories in all forms. When writing, she tends to stick to short stories and graphic novels, and most of her works are speculative in nature.

Elyse has had works accepted with *Mermaid's Monthly*, *Hyphen Punk*, *Crone Girl's Press*, *Outcast Press*, *Markosia*, *Last Girls Club*, and more. Her horror graphic novella, *The Fell Witch*, is an allegory for postpartum depression and will be released in 2022 with Band of Bards comics.

When not writing, Elyse enjoys long naps with her cats, reading, and donuts. Also cheese. Learn more about her works and world at her website: *elyserussellauthor.squarespace.com*.

# YOU MIGHT ALSO ENJOY

### THE ALCHEMIST DAUGHTER
by Paul S. Moore

*When a concoction of ethers channels a little of their magic properties to one location, inspiration springs to life.*

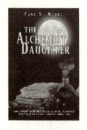

### PARRISH BLUE
by Vanessa MacLaren-Wray

*Sallie never expected to discover a world she'd forgotten how to imagine.*

### THE THIRD TIME'S THE CHARM
by Steven D. Brewer

*When an airship is hijacked by pirates, a young man with a secret loses his mentor ... and his future.*

Available in digital and trade paperback editions from
Water Dragon Publishing
*waterdragonpublishing.com/dragongems*

CPSIA information can be obtained
at www.ICGtesting.com
Printed in the USA
JSHW040227191022
31826JS00002B/67